First published 1989 by Walker Books Ltd
87 Vauxhall Walk, London SE11 5HJ

This edition published 2008

4 6 8 10 9 7 5 3

© 1989 Nick Butterworth

The right of Nick Butterworth to be identified as
author/illustrator of this work has been asserted by him in accordance
with the Copyright, Designs and Patents Act 1988

This book has been typeset in New Century School Book

Printed in China

British Library Cataloguing in Publication Data:
a catalogue record for this book is available from the British Library

ISBN 978-1-4063-1242-3

www.walkerbooks.co.uk

My Mum is FANTASTIC

Nick Butterworth

WALKER BOOKS
AND SUBSIDIARIES
LONDON • BOSTON • SYDNEY • AUCKLAND

My mum is
fantastic.

She's a
brilliant artist ...

and she can
balance on a
tightrope …

and she can
mend anything …

and she tells
the most exciting
stories …

and she's
a fantastic
gardener …

and she can
swim like a
fish ...

and she can do
amazing stunts
on a bike ...

and she can
knit anything …

and she can
tame wild
animals …

and she makes
the best parties
in the world.

It's great to
have a mum
like mine.

It's fantastic!

Other titles by Nick Butterworth

ISBN 978-4063-1330-7   ISBN 978-1-4063-1243-0   ISBN 978-4063-1331-4

"I wonder how much time I spent as a boy singing the praises of my family.
My grandpa could make *anything* out of *anything*. My grandma was the
best friend anyone could ever wish for. My dad was little short of Superman
and my mum ... well, perhaps she actually *was* Wonderwoman!
It's heartening to know that children feel the same today
as I did then. Especially my own two!"

NICK BUTTERWORTH

Available from all good bookstores

www.walkerbooks.co.uk